First published in Great Britain 2017 by Egmont UK Limited
The Yellow Building, 1 Nicholas Road, London W11 4AN

Illustrations by Ulises Farinas
Color by Gabriel Cassata
Written by Katrina Pallant
Designed by Richie Hull

Published by Phoenix International Publications, Inc.
8501 West Higgins Road   59 Gloucester Place
Chicago, Illinois 60631   London W1U 8JJ

p i kids is a trademark of Phoenix International Publications, Inc.,
and is registered in the United States.
Look and Find is a trademark of
Phoenix International Publications, Inc.,
and is registered in the United States and Canada.

www.pikidsmedia.com

Printed In Canada.

8 7 6 5 4 3 2 1

ISBN: 978-1-5037-2577-5

STAR WARS™
WHERE'S THE WOOKIEE? 2

Look and Find®

pi kids **Phoenix International Publications, Inc.**

Chicago • London • New York • Hamburg • Mexico City • Paris • Sydney

WULLFFWARRO

TARFFUL

BLACK KRRSANTAN

CHEWBACCA

CHALPAL

GUNGI

FIND THIS WOOKIEE!

Chewbacca is hiding in every location. But watch out! This time he has brought some fur-covered friends. See how many of these hairy giants are in each location:

RORJOW

CHALKAZZA

LOHGARRA

ULIBACCA

LOCATIONS

Raarrwwr ararrrrr

The hairy hero has been spotted across the galaxy, joined by rebel allies for you to find. But beware! The following locations also hide enemies from the Empire and the First Order:

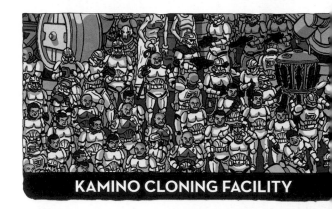

KAMINO CLONING FACILITY

DROID FACTORY

OTOH GUNGA

LOTHAL

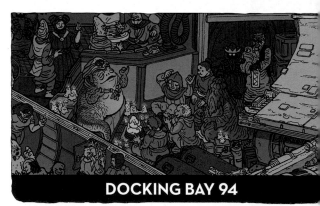

DOCKING BAY 94

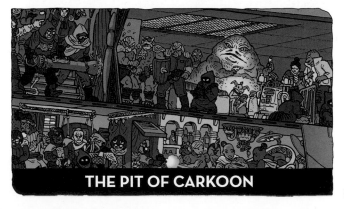

THE PIT OF CARKOON

HOME ONE

JEDHA

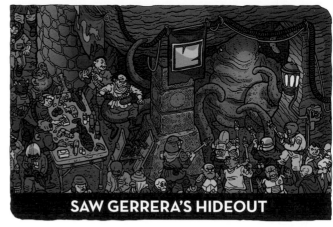

SAW GERRERA'S HIDEOUT

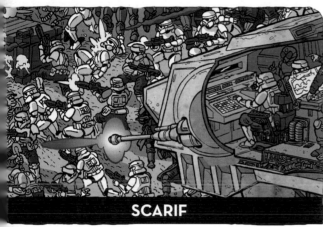

SCARIF

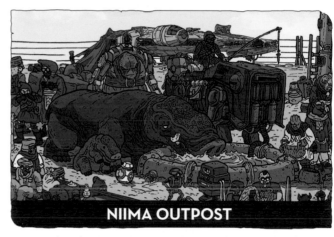

NIIMA OUTPOST

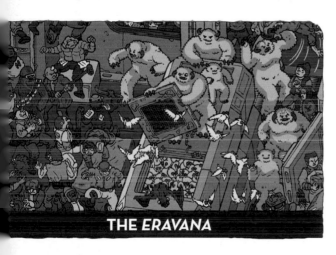

THE *ERAVANA*

MAZ KANATA'S CASTLE

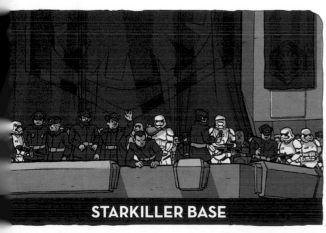

STARKILLER BASE

RESISTANCE BASE

KAMINO CLONING FACILITY

On an aquatic planet south of the Rishi Maze lives a tall, elegant race called the Kaminoans. They are well known for their cloning technology and are tasked with building an army vitally important to the Galactic Republic.

OBI-WAN KENOBI   **99**   **ASAJJ VENTRESS**   **GENERAL GRIEVOUS**   **JANGO FETT**   **YOUNG BOBA FETT**

DROID FACTORY

The Geonosians are a technologically advanced species, making their homeworld an ideal place for a massive battle droid foundry. Each facility houses hundreds of conveyor belts capable of creating thousands of droids a day.

COUNT DOOKU	POGGLE THE LESSER	R2-D2	C-3PO	WAT TAMBOR	SHU MAI

OTOH GUNGA

Beneath the waters of Naboo lies a city of bubbles, a series of buildings created by the amphibious Gungans. They are a proud warrior race that, despite their peaceful nature, would do anything to protect their home.

JAR JAR BINKS · PADMÉ AMIDALA · RISH LOO · AHSOKA · ANAKIN SKYWALKER · BOSS NASS

LOTHAL

A planet in the Outer Rim territories, Lothal was in such economic hardship that its people invited the Empire with open arms. Now disillusioned with their oppressors, some Lothalites welcome the appearance of rebel cells, black-market activity, and all-out resistance to the Imperial regime.

HERA   EZRA   KANAN   SABINE   INQUISITOR   CHOPPER

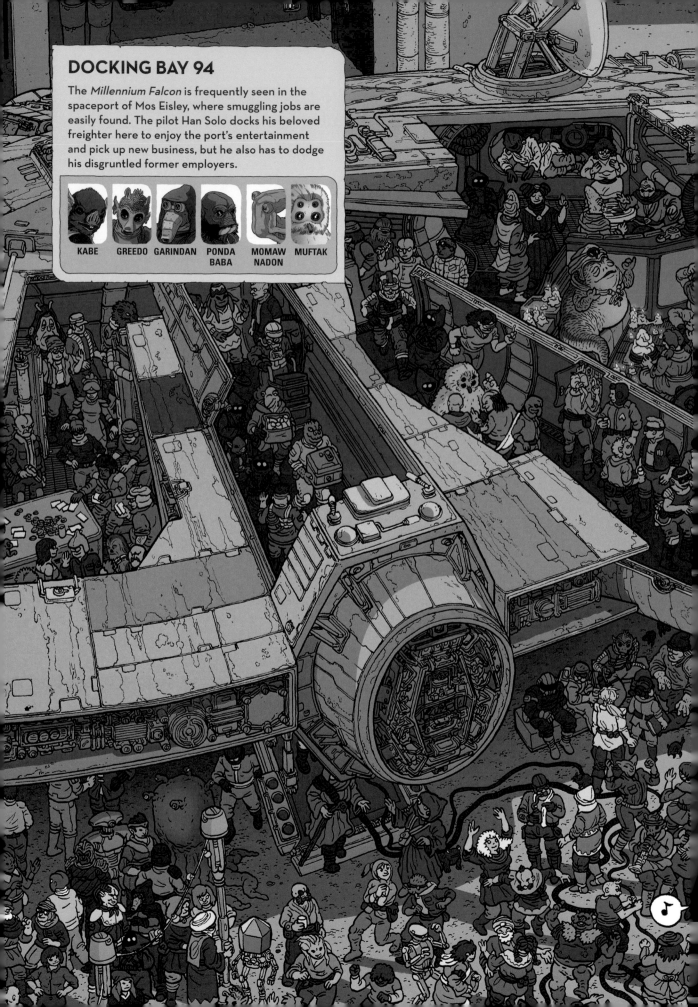

DOCKING BAY 94

The *Millennium Falcon* is frequently seen in the spaceport of Mos Eisley, where smuggling jobs are easily found. The pilot Han Solo docks his beloved freighter here to enjoy the port's entertainment and pick up new business, but he also has to dodge his disgruntled former employers.

KABE **GREEDO** **GARINDAN** **PONDA BABA** **MOMAW NADON** **MUFTAK**

THE PIT OF CARKOON

In the desert of Tatooine lies a giant pit, which is home to a terrifying creature known as the sarlacc. Crime lord Jabba the Hutt uses the pit to frighten his enemies. He frequently visits it aboard his sail barge, the *Khetanna*.

HAN SOLO   **BOBA FETT**   **BIB FORTUNA**   **BOUSHH**   **MAX REBO**   **EV-9D9**

HOME ONE

Home One was originally built to explore deep space, but now serves as a military vessel and is armed with ion cannons, turbolasers, and several tractor beams. This star cruiser is the largest and most advanced ship in the Alliance fleet, making it a crucial base of operations for the rebel cause.

PRINCESS LEIA **GENERAL MADINE** **WEDGE ANTILLES** **2-1B** **LANDO CALRISSIAN** **NIEN NUNB**

JEDHA

This ancient desert moon is rich in kyber crystals, and therefore of great significance to the Empire. Though occupied by Imperial forces, the deeply spiritual people of Jedha continue to worship the Force and welcome pilgrims to the Holy City.

SILVANIE PHEST   KULLBEE SPERADO   WEETEEF   K-2SO   BEEZER FORTUNA   MOROFF

SAW GERRERA'S HIDEOUT

Coordinating a rebellion against the occupying forces on Jedha, Saw Gerrera is a familiar face in the fight against the Empire. Now bunkered down in his secluded caves, Saw has his gang of rebels carry out brutal missions to destabilize the regime.

| G2-1B7 | CYCYED OCK | LEEVAN TENZA | MAGVA YARRO | EDRIO | SAW GERRERA |

SCARIF

This remote tropical planet is home to an Imperial military base with a terrifying secret. The facility is being used to construct a planet-destroying superweapon, the Death Star. Scarif is protected by a deflector shield, but it can be entered—and data can be transmitted—through a shield gate...

JYN   CASSIAN   BAZE   CHIRRUT   BODHI   KRENNIC

NIIMA OUTPOST

Jakku is an ideal place for scavengers, due to its many shipwrecks from a long-ago battle between the Empire and Rebellion. The ruthless Unkar Plutt has a stronghold on the settlement where these scavengers come to trade their finds.

REY   **BB-8**   **UNKAR PLUTT**   **SARCO PLANK**   **LOR SAN TEKKA**   **BOBBAJO**

THE *ERAVANA*

After losing the *Millennium Falcon*, Han and Chewie came into possession of a large heavy freighter and used it to resume their smuggling career. The *Eravana* is not well-armed, nor is it as fast as the *Falcon*, but it does have the space for a lot of strange cargo, including frightening livestock.

FINN

HAN SOLO

TASU LEECH

REY

BALA-TIK

BB-8

MAZ KANATA'S CASTLE

On the planet Takodana lives a pirate queen who allows smugglers to reside in her ancient castle. Maz has strict rules against violence, so travelers from across the galaxy can find refuge here from bounty hunters and political enemies.

MAZ KANATA **HAN SOLO** **CRIMSON CORSAIR** **GRUMMGAR** **BAZINE NETAL** **ME-8D9**

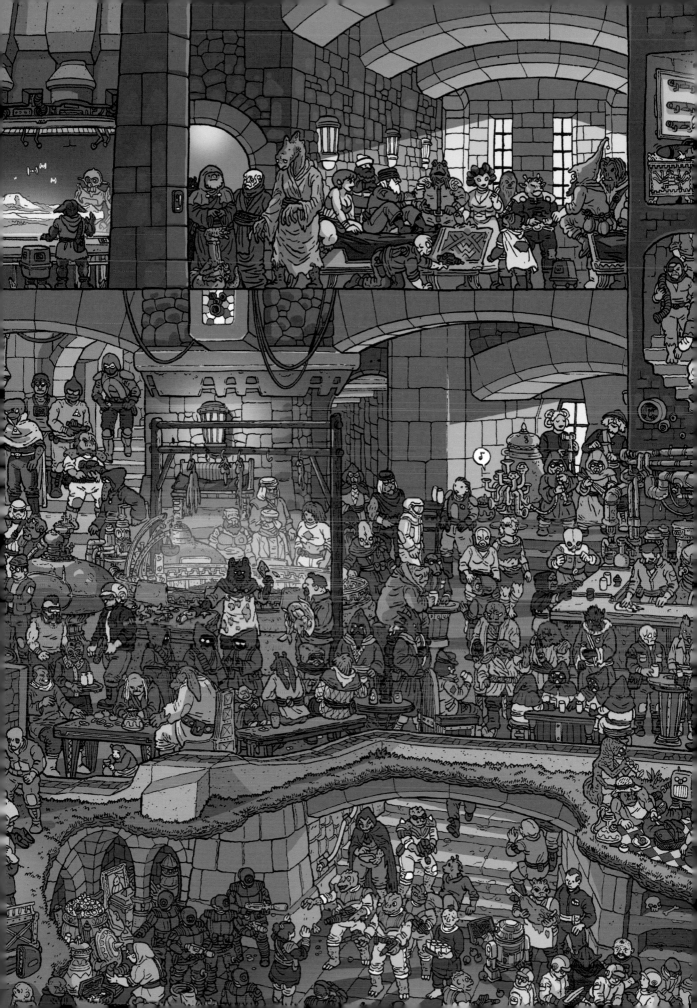

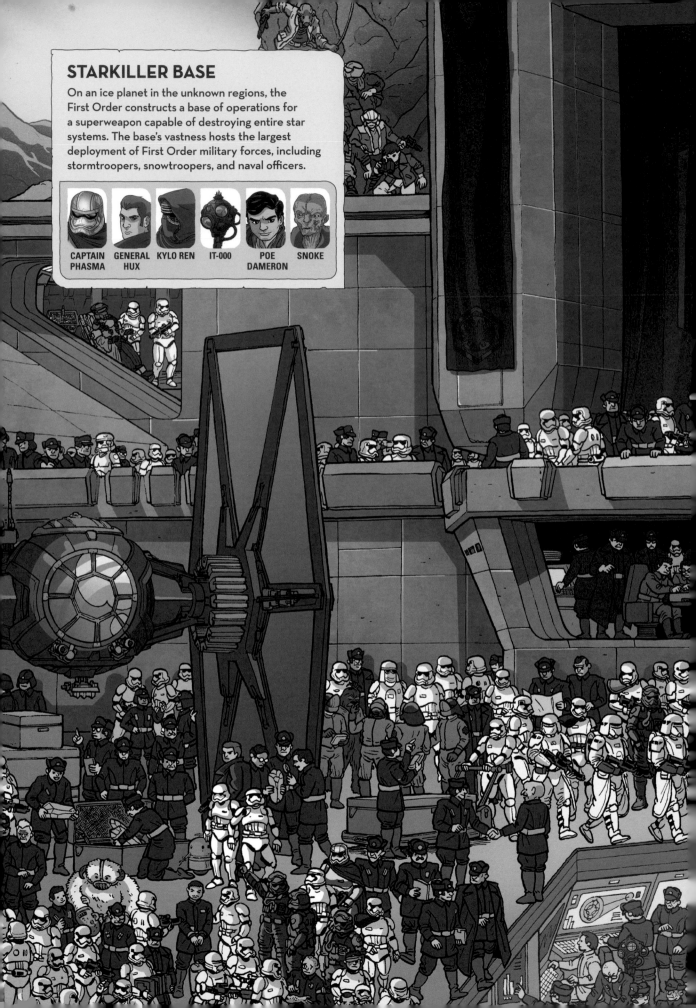

STARKILLER BASE

On an ice planet in the unknown regions, the First Order constructs a base of operations for a superweapon capable of destroying entire star systems. The base's vastness hosts the largest deployment of First Order military forces, including stormtroopers, snowtroopers, and naval officers.

CAPTAIN PHASMA · GENERAL HUX · KYLO REN · IT-000 · POE DAMERON · SNOKE

RESISTANCE BASE

The Resistance headquarters is surrounded by thick jungle and the command center is underground, meaning the facility is well-concealed from enemy sensors. Multiple hangars hold the Resistance Fleet, including the all-important X-wings.

POE DAMERON

ELLO ASTY

GENERAL ORGANA

FINN

NIEN NUNB

PZ-4CO

GALACTIC CHECKLIST

These might be a bit harder to find...

KAMINO CLONING FACILITY

- [ ] detached AT-TE laser cannon
- [ ] trooper with artificial eye
- [ ] protocol droid
- [ ] Kylo Ren's helmet
- [ ] trooper looking through a periscope
- [ ] trooper with a beard
- [ ] flying trooper in red armor
- [ ] Kaminoan riding an aiwha

DROID FACTORY

- [ ] battle droid of a different color
- [ ] discarded assassin droid
- [ ] exploding battle droid
- [ ] giant beetle
- [ ] Viceroy Nute Gunray
- [ ] Twi'lek with a lightsaber
- [ ] battle droid with different head
- [ ] three-legged droid

OTOH GUNGA

- [ ] Gungan walking a lobster
- [ ] colo claw fish
- [ ] Admiral Ackbar
- [ ] Gungan carrying fruit
- [ ] Gungan playing a drum
- [ ] Gungan with a pink waistcoat
- [ ] kaadu

LOTHAL

- [ ] group of Quarren
- [ ] mechanic under speeder
- [ ] Bith inspecting crystals on sale
- [ ] Biths in a window
- [ ] girl trying on rebel helmet
- [ ] carpet seller
- [ ] brain in a jar
- [ ] thirsty birds

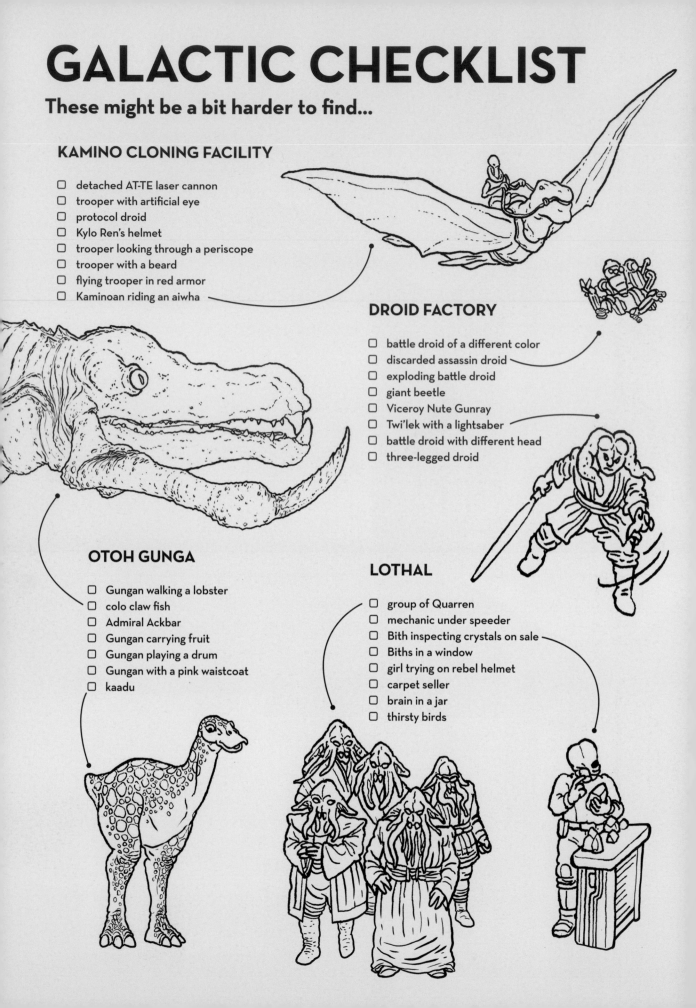

OCKING BAY 94

- barbecue
- Rodian playing a horn
- droid DJ
- Toong
- carrots
- X-wing pilot
- sleeping Ewok
- two Toydarians

THE PIT OF CARKOON

- ☐ Gamorrean caught by the Sarlacc
- ☐ spit roast
- ☐ baby Hutt
- ☐ Bossk
- ☐ dewback
- ☐ battering ram
- ☐ Salacious B. Crumb
- ☐ herd of banthas

HOME ONE

- ☐ thermos
- ☐ Rodian pilot
- ☐ pilot writing a letter
- ☐ red rebel pilot helmet
- ☐ Death Star II hologram
- ☐ air traffic controller
- ☐ Aqualish officers
- ☐ buzz droid

JEDHA

- ☐ brown bird
- ☐ Brotherhood of the Beatific Countenance
- ☐ red R2 unit
- ☐ tank being pelted with fruit
- ☐ man getting drenched by bucket of water
- ☐ fruit seller
- ☐ man with eye patch
- ☐ alien rebel pilot

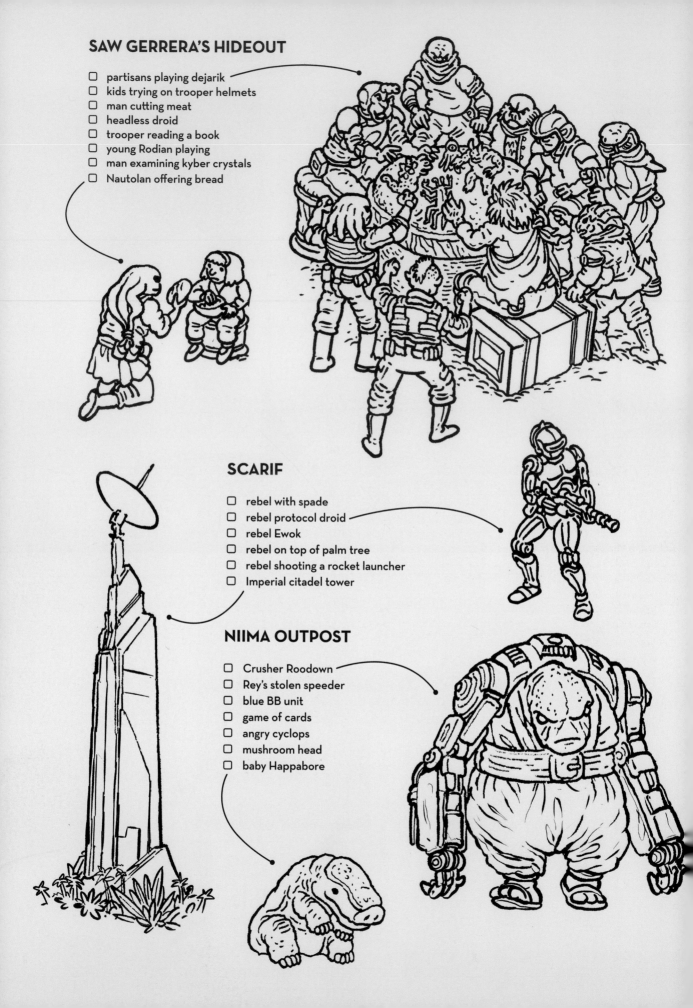

SAW GERRERA'S HIDEOUT

- ☐ partisans playing dejarik
- ☐ kids trying on trooper helmets
- ☐ man cutting meat
- ☐ headless droid
- ☐ trooper reading a book
- ☐ young Rodian playing
- ☐ man examining kyber crystals
- ☐ Nautolan offering bread

SCARIF

- ☐ rebel with spade
- ☐ rebel protocol droid
- ☐ rebel Ewok
- ☐ rebel on top of palm tree
- ☐ rebel shooting a rocket launcher
- ☐ Imperial citadel tower

NIIMA OUTPOST

- ☐ Crusher Roodown
- ☐ Rey's stolen speeder
- ☐ blue BB unit
- ☐ game of cards
- ☐ angry cyclops
- ☐ mushroom head
- ☐ baby Happabore

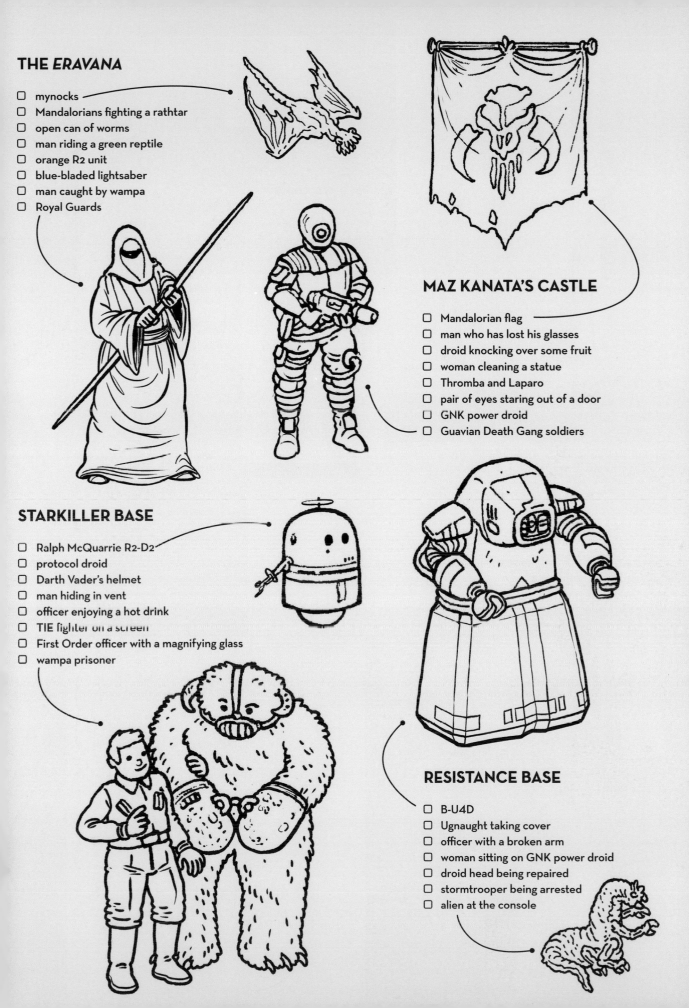

THE *ERAVANA*

- ☐ mynocks
- ☐ Mandalorians fighting a rathtar
- ☐ open can of worms
- ☐ man riding a green reptile
- ☐ orange R2 unit
- ☐ blue-bladed lightsaber
- ☐ man caught by wampa
- ☐ Royal Guards

MAZ KANATA'S CASTLE

- ☐ Mandalorian flag
- ☐ man who has lost his glasses
- ☐ droid knocking over some fruit
- ☐ woman cleaning a statue
- ☐ Thromba and Laparo
- ☐ pair of eyes staring out of a door
- ☐ GNK power droid
- ☐ Guavian Death Gang soldiers

STARKILLER BASE

- ☐ Ralph McQuarrie R2-D2
- ☐ protocol droid
- ☐ Darth Vader's helmet
- ☐ man hiding in vent
- ☐ officer enjoying a hot drink
- ☐ TIE fighter on a screen
- ☐ First Order officer with a magnifying glass
- ☐ wampa prisoner

RESISTANCE BASE

- ☐ B-U4D
- ☐ Ugnaught taking cover
- ☐ officer with a broken arm
- ☐ woman sitting on GNK power droid
- ☐ droid head being repaired
- ☐ stormtrooper being arrested
- ☐ alien at the console